Doctor Rabbit's Foundling

by
Jan Wahl

ILLUSTRATED BY CYNDY SZEKERES

Pantheon Books

for Jan and Rosite

Leaves were wet in the path.

Sun-up's morning mist
blew over the river.
Ferns glistened with dew.

Crocuses shone like lamps
lighting Doctor Rabbit's
way.

Screech Owl had twisted her claw.
The Doctor set it
and now was sprinting along home.

He almost stumbled

over a tiny bamboo bucket.

There was a note.

Take care of my child.

Signed:

The Unhappy Mother.

At first

there seemed to be nothing inside.

Until

Doctor Rabbit saw a VERY

small tadpole

swimming around.

Small as it was,

it had wonderful eyes!

He carried it back home with him.

Soon word spread.

"A child was found!"

Every hour the Doctor slipped

into the nursery

to gaze at the bed.

Tadpole grew by the minute.

Patients brought Hot

Leaf Pie, Lettuce Pudding,

Radish Tapioca.

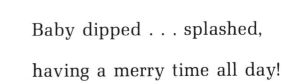

Baby dipped . . . splashed,

having a merry time all day!

Fast legs began sprouting

where the tail was.

Miss Mouse would sing

it to sleep

SOFTLY SOFTLY.

Now it had little toes and feet.

Doctor Rabbit would creep in,

proudly admiring it.

Baby's eyes were bright-beautiful.

Sparkling gold,

black-centered!

He called *her*

Tiny Toad.

Suddenly front legs popped out.

Now she could hold a rattle

given by Raccoon.

"GRR-KK" was her first word.
Miss Mouse told the
Doctor who called in
his patients.

Tiny Toad hopped
her first hop.
Blip!
They cheered.

After that, it was difficult

to keep her in her carriage.

Bor-RUNGG!!

Tiny Toad might leap anywhere.

In the sugar bowl!

On the

medicine shelf!

Blup! Baroom!

Up in a geranium plant

where she slipped off a leaf.

She slept on his pillow.

In the middle of the Night
Doctor Rabbit heard
her leaping about the
room.

Then—*bor*-RUNGG—
she'd hop to the window,
staring at the dark.

She listened to Night

sounds of crickets

and cicadas, her eyes two

huge, rolling moons.

Finally he let her out.

But he lay awake

waiting for her return.

And when she did, he fell asleep.

Doctor Rabbit sent
for his mother.

It was impossible
for him to watch
Tiny Toad
day *and* night.

Mother Rabbit was quick

at catching the

Foundling on warm

afternoons when

Tiny played in the cool shade

of rhubarb stalks.

However,

each evening

when the Sun

fell below the western rim,

Tiny Toad would not stay in bed.

Her thoughts were

of other things—

Ants, snails, and slugs.

One Night Tiny heard

other toads singing.

Doctor Rabbit sat with his mother

and Miss Mouse

in starlight,

smelling jasmine

and wild roses.

Nervously Tiny hopped.

Blip, blup, blip!

Doctor Rabbit tried playing

a banjo to

keep her home.

Tiny Toad gave them a long,

last look with her

marvelous eyes, then

hopped—hopped—

hopped—

Out of sight—

into the Night noises.

"She is going just as you

left me, Son," sighed

Mother Rabbit.

"As every child must

go away at last."

"Yes, Mama," he whispered.

But his eyes flickered with tears.